Other books by Sue Patton Thoele

Autumn of the Spring Chicken
Heart Centered Marriage
The Courage to Be Yourself
The Woman's Book of Confidence
The Woman's Book of Courage

The Courage *to* Be Yourself Journal

Created by
SUE PATTON THOELE

CONARI PRESS
Berkeley, California

All selections are from THE COURAGE TO BE YOURSELF.
© Copyright 1988, 1991 by Sue Patton Thoele.

Printed in the United States of America

Conari Press books are distributed by Publishers Group West

Cover design: Leigh Wells
Cover illustration: Rae Ecklund
Book design: Suzanne Albertson

ISBN: 1-57324-065-6

10 9 8 7 6 5 4 3 2 1

Introduction

It takes an enormous amount of courage to be who we truly are. Thankfully, women are innately courageous. Whether we realize it or not, each day we act and speak courageously.

Although we may inherently have the courage to be ourselves, we also need to know who we are. One of the best ways to become aware of, and remain connected to, who we uniquely are is to develop the habit of journaling. The practice of writing intimately to and about ourselves helps us become conscious of the vital trait of courage within us. It also acts as a continual, personal conversation with ourselves in which we can reveal our authenticity and cultivate a deep, committed relationship with our dear friend, self. For, contrary to what we may think, being our own close and constant friend is not selfish or self-centered. It is, indeed, one of the most effective ways of freeing ourselves from limiting fears and beliefs.

Journaling is a great way to become aware of all our feelings—whether painful and imprisoning or joyful and exhilarating. And as we awaken to all our emotions, we can then acknowledge and accept them. We then become better able to transform those feelings that keep us stuck, and celebrate those that represent the core of who we are. Mining the treasures to be found within ourselves through journaling helps us fall in love with our real selves and become increasingly gifted at giving genuine, unconditional love to those with whom we share either solitary moments or our entire lives.

Depending on the circumstances of my life, my journal has played the part of safe confidante, grief counselor, recipient of my rage, and conduit for hearing the soft whispers of soul. It's my hope that your time with this journal will bear the fruit of a deepening friendship with yourself and an ever-increasing feeling of authenticity. May it help light the lamps of courage along your path.

Framing our lives
with slices of
solitude gives us a
richer sense of self
and greater peace
of mind.

Courage is the
ability to do what
needs to be done, or
feel what needs
to be felt, in spite
of fear.

Give yourself the gift
of ten minutes a day
just for you—ten
minutes of silence
and contemplation.

The most important
connection I can
make is with myself.
From that connect-
ing grows my ability
to be free and to
love.

Being emotionally
independent doesn't
mean that we're
selfish, self-centered,
or unavailable to
others. It means that
we're centered in an
awareness of who
we are—no longer
fragmented by fear
or unrealistic
demands from our-
selves or others.

Healthy emotional
independence is our
birthright, our
privilege, and our
responsibility.

Being ourselves is
often not easy, but
it is essential for
evolution and soul
growth.

Be patient with yourself as you continue your journey toward being who you authentically are. Don't try to go it alone.

We need to talk to
ourselves gently and
with love.

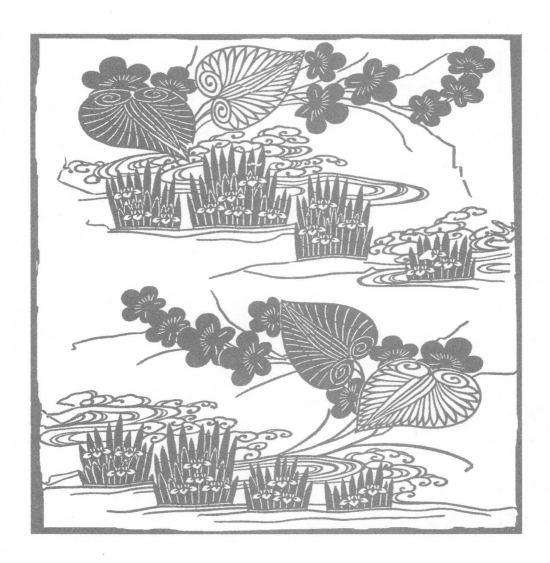

Bringing our fears
out into the open
and talking honestly
about them helps us
work through them.
An unspoken fear is
much more powerful
than one that is
shared.

When we are really
solid in our belief
that we don't need to
submit to unaccept-
able treatment, and
state our limit clearly,
it will probably stop.

When *we* change,
our relationships also
begin to change.

When we attach our-
selves to the role of
mothering another
adult, we usurp their
right to learn from
their mistakes and
poison the relation-
ship between us.

As we find the
courage to allow our-
selves to be who we
are—imperfect, but
committed to
improvement—we
begin to untie the
ropes that bind
us to emotional
dependence.

We all need security,
but security obtained
at the expense of
exhilarating, creative
growth and change
merely strangles us.

We may not be able
to change events, but
we *can* change our
reaction to them.

The first and most
basic step for any
change or growth,
no matter how small,
is to know what we
feel, how we think,
and how we would
like to alter our lives.

We all need to feel understood and con-nected to others. In a climate of nonjudg-mental love, we can truly become who we are meant to be.

Using words such as *should* and *have to* implies that we have no power to choose in the matter. It's good to replace them with will and choose to—words that free us to make conscious choices.

Accepting our feel-
ings exactly as they
are provides an inner
climate that's con-
ducive to growth
and change.

Feelings are neither
right nor wrong—
they just are.

Accepting and
forgiving ourselves
creates a mood in
which we find it
easier to forgive and
accept others.

Having the courage
to search for the
source of our fears is
a necessary first step
toward being who we
really are, free from
limitations and able
to live our lives to
our fullest potential.

Consciously or
unconsciously, we
teach people how
to treat us.

Appeasing behavior
comes from a fearful,
powerless place
inside of us, a place
where there is very
little choice.
Conscious compro-
mise springs from
our empowered self,
the part of us that
knows we have the
right and the ability
to choose.

Our freedom diminishes when we are afraid of standing up to others.

An essential part
of a happy, healthy
life is being of ser-
vice to others; but
being indispensable
is destructive.

Talking to others
about our feelings is
very helpful in
resolving that old
gremlin, guilt. It's
amazing how quickly
guilt can melt away
when we receive
loving feedback from
other people who,
because they're less
involved, can be
more objective about
what's happening
to us.

Many of our accom-
plishments happen in
spite of fear.

It's tempting to ignore our anger in order not to rock the boat; but to resolve it wisely, we need to pay attention to it.

We can never make people happy or successful. By feeling that we must make people happy, we merely set ourselves up for inevitable disappointment.

The good news
about learned fear
is that it can be
unlearned.

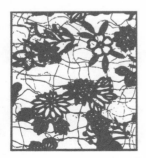

We have a right to
be angry; but with
that right comes the
responsibility to
express our anger
constructively.

In order to heal and
become our authen-
tic selves, we must
recognize and
unravel the pain of
grief when it winds
itself around our
hearts.

Change is action; old habits are reactions. To change and transform, we must consciously choose new actions.

Time is a healer and,
though it may hardly
seem possible while
we grieve, if we
allow ourselves to
move through grief,
we will heal.

Choose and *love* may
be the two most
empowering and
life-changing words
we can make our
own on a day-to-day
basis.

Before acting, pause!
Take a time out—a
literal breather—to
gain perspective.

Listen to what you're
saying to yourself in
the privacy of your
own mind. If what
you habitually tell
yourself is optimistic,
uplifting, and loving,
you're certain to
be a person who
feels happy and
energized.

The way to transform
inner saboteurs is to
learn to love, accept,
and understand our-
selves as we are.

We need to plan for the future, but not worry. Planning creates security; worry creates pain.

Our feelings, and
the thoughts that
created them, are our
own responsibility,
nobody else's.

Probably the most important affirmation we can use is: *I love myself.* If you simply can't say that, try: *I'm willing to love myself,* or, *I'm willing to be willing to love myself.*

What we think we
are, we will become.

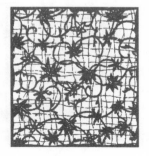

Before we can expect
to be treated well,
we must believe that
we deserve good
treatment.

Growth requires the
ability and willing-
ness to risk, to court
the unexpected, no
matter how scary
that may be.

It's up to us: We can
believe in our limita-
tions, or we can
choose to believe
that we can soar.

Every risk we take in
our journey toward
being completely
ourselves makes
it easier for others
to summon the
courage to risk
being themselves.

We need to learn to
communicate with
the goal of under-
standing each other;
speaking without
blaming and listen-
ing without judging.

There are many
things in our lives
over which we have
no control and for
which we aren't
responsible; but we
are responsible for
how we respond to
any circumstance.

Listening is probably
the most important
part of any communi-
cation with ourselves
and with others.

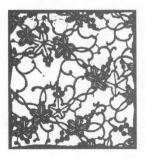

We have the right to
honor what we want
and need, and have
others do so also.

Resistance magnifies pain by causing tension; tension creates tightness, stiffness, inflexibility; and being stiff, tight, and inflexible makes us vulnerable. In high winds, better the yielding willow than the resisting oak.

Growth and personal
unfolding begin
when we give our-
selves permission
to *be*.

It is essential that we bring balance and harmony into our lives by investing energy in each of the four areas of our being: emotional, physical, mental, and spiritual.

We are worthy
of love. We do
deserve our own
and others' support
and friendship.

It's so important that
we learn to forgive
ourselves as readily
as we do a beloved
child or friend.

A healthy source of
support cares about
our pain but does
not carry it for us or
try to cure it.

The courage to be
yourself is a quest,
more easily accom-
plished in a climate
of tolerance, accep-
tance, and flexibility.

All our opportunities beckon us from the center of this present moment. *Today* we can improve on our choices, stand up for our rights, and befriend ourselves.

A wise and wonderful woman once told me, "The future depends on a healed past and a well-lived present."

I have the courage
to embrace my
strengths and be
gentle with my
weaknesses.

We need to add the
zest of enthusiasm to
our days and allow
ourselves to get
excited about life.

Mother God, help
me to be Loving.
Father God, help me
to be Useful.
Mother/Father God,
help me to be Me;
a unique and
valuable expression
of You.

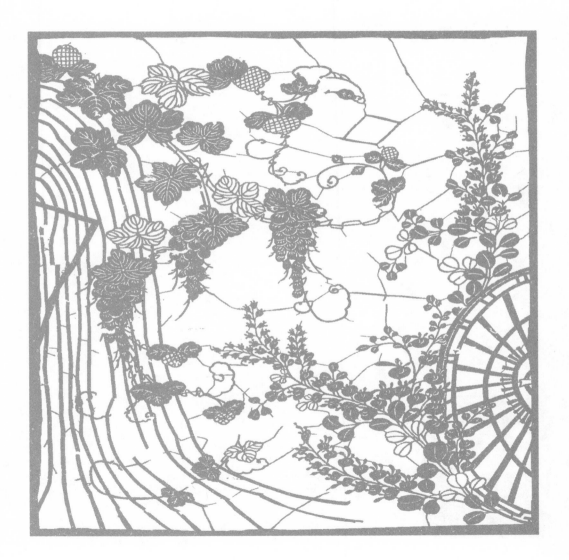

One of the best
things we can do for
ourselves is to have
realistic expectations
of ourselves and
others.

Live gently with
yourself and others.

Personal Note

If *The Courage to Be Yourself Journal* feels like a helpful friend to you, then, both as a woman and a writer, I am very happy. As we find the courage to embark on the sometimes frightening path towards increased authenticity, we all need hands to hold. Through this book maybe we can, in effect, hold each others' hands. May your journey be filled with the laughter of a healed inner child, a rainbow of miracles, and a close communion with your Goddess within.

If you have ideas or experiences you would like to share, or if you would like to purchase autographed copies of any of my books, please write to me:

Sue Patton Thoele
P.O. Box 1519
Boulder, CO 80306-1519

Conari Press, established in 1987, publishes books on topics
ranging from spirituality and women's history to sexuality and
personal growth. Our main goal is to publish quality books
that will make a difference in people's lives—both
how we feel about ourselves and how
we relate to one another.

Our readers are our most important resource, and we
value your input, suggestions, and ideas. We'd love to hear
from you—after all, we are publishing
books for you!

For a complete catalog or to get on our mailing list,
please contact us at:

CONARI PRESS
2550 Ninth Street, Suite 101
Berkeley, CA 94710

800•685•9595   Fax 510•649•7190
e-mail: Conaripub@aol.com